LOOKOUT
POINT

CHARITY

THE ILAS

LADYFACE

LABYRINTH

ILA VISTA

PARADISE
COVE

GENERAL STORE

Toys

CANDY

KNOTTY PINE

SCHOOL HOUSE

FIRESIDE

# Welcome to the World of

WILLOWBE WOODS

## Campfire Stories

WANDERING
ROAD

# A Team Of One

Written by
## Ila Wallen

Illustrated by
## Robert Sauber

Willowbe Woods Campfire Stories
Created by
## Bill Wallen & Ila Wallen

# A Golden Book • New York

Bill Wallen—Publisher and Art Director
Michael Wallen—Designer and Graphic Art Production
Patrick Davidson—Editorial Director • Carolyn Wallen and Christine Oliver—Editors
Laurine DiRocco—Educational Consultant
The Willowbe Woods Campfire Stories were created by Bill Wallen and Ila Wallen.

*Library of Congress Cataloging-in-Publication Data*
Wallen, Ila
A team of one / written by Ila Wallen; illustrated by Robert Sauber
p. cm.—(Willowbe Woods campfire stories)—"A Golden Book."
Summary: Papa Rango, reading to the animals in the Willowbe Woods, shares the story of how Bandit the raccoon learned how to work as part of a team.
ISBN 0-375-82705-6
[1. Cooperativeness—Fiction. 2. Treasure hunts—Fiction. 3. Raccoons—Fiction. 4. Animals—Fiction. 5. Stories in rhyme.] I. Sauber, Rob, ill. II. Title.
III. Series: Wallen, Ila. Willowbe Woods campfire stories.
PZ8.3.W168Te 2004      [E]—dc22      2003012493

www.goldenbooks.com
Printed in the United States of America
First Random House Edition 2004
10 9 8 7 6 5 4 3 2 1

2

To my children Ryan and Ava,
for showing me hidden treasures
in life's big scavenger hunt
—Ila Wallen

To my daughter Sophia's treasured
grandparents, Baba and Dedo
—Robert Sauber

On a journey we'll go! Come follow me
To the enchanted woods of Willowbe.

Laughter and warmth surround the campfire
In Willowbe Woods, where stories inspire.

Papa Rango greets friends from far and near
With happy hugs and a welcoming cheer.

The Willowbeings gather every night,
Sharing stories by the campfire light.

Bent Willow recalls each tale that is told.
Her leaves remember stories new and old.

Papa Rango opens his book with care
And asks, "Tonight, whose story shall I share?"

5

The kids' voices are loud; they're in such a hurry!
Hands fly up in the air with a frenzied flurry.
Papa Rango walks round, tapping one on the head,
And that Willowbeing's cheeks turn strawberry red.

It's Bandit, the raccoon, his mouth open wide.
Being picked is a surprise he cannot hide.

"Do you mean the time when I didn't want to play
And share in the teamwork on scavenger hunt day?"

"That's the one, Bandit," Papa Rango says with delight.
He begins reading, "Once upon a Willowbe night . . ."

7

Charity had set up a fun
game to play . . .

A scavenger hunt that would
take them all day.

"Please find all the things on
the list I gave you;

Then come back to me when
your searching is through."

8

"Hey," said Bandit, "we're the scavenger hunt crew.
These pictures are great. This will be fun to do!"

Will asked, "Do you think we can find all these things?"
"Of course," said Bunny. "We are Willowbeings!"

9

A washboard, a wagon, and a silver shell.
Two crayons, a coconut, and a cowbell.

Some hair spray, a toy truck, and one
bright red shoe.

A whistle, paintbrushes, and
blueberry goo.

A trash can, a doorknob, an old wooden clock,
  Ten wood chips, two tires, and one orange sock.

A fishing pole, a key, and a telephone,
  And last on the list, a large rainbow pinecone.

Flynn sniffed the air, his long
nose leading the way
To find the paintbrushes and
bottle of hair spray.

Bandit searched all over for
the silver shell,
But Will found it first inside
the wishing well.

Sophie perked up her ears and led the group of five
To find a hidden wagon that they could all drive.

Bandit ran to the bridge for the pieces of wood,
But Bunny got to them much faster than he could.

**W**ill searched high and low and finally had some luck
When under a bush he found the little toy truck.

**B**andit looked for the blueberries all over town,
But Sophie was the one who quickly tracked them down.

Bandit said to himself,
"I won't play anymore.
Wherever I look, someone has
been there before!"

He told his friends what
he was going to do.
"I can search by myself,
without all of you."

15

Finding things was easy now that Bandit was only one.

**W**ith no one to compete with, he was having lots of fun.

17

While on his search for the whistle and key,
Bandit was feeling a little lonely.

"Although the game is fun and I'm doing well,
Sharing it with a friend would really be swell."

Bandit found his friends playing along Wandering Road.
He was shocked at the size of their scavenger hunt load.

Bandit watched them work together, laughing as they played,
And with a frown on his face, he sadly walked away.

19

Bandit realized he was bored from searching on his own.
"I don't even want to find that silly old pinecone.

My backpack is heavy, and stuff's spilling on the floor."
He yelled out in frustration, "It's not fun anymore!"

Bandit heard voices, and through the bushes he could see
His friends gathering in the shade of Knotty Pine Tree.

He listened closely to his friends talk about their day.
Bandit was surprised when he heard what they had to say.

"I wish Bandit
wanted to
play with us."

"Who knows
why he made
such a big fuss?"

"We never let
him have a
turn to play."

"I really
missed my
friend Bandit
today."

21

"They do miss me," said Bandit. "I thought they didn't care.
It's my fault I'm not with them. I didn't want to share.

I need to tell my friends about what I have learned.
A good team works together, and we all take a turn."

Leaping through the bushes and surprising the group of four,
Bandit yelled, "We don't need to miss each other anymore.
I never would have left you all if I had only known
The lesson I learned today by being on my own.

It's not about who can be the fastest or the best
But how we learn to share in the scavenger hunt quest.
It was lonely searching when I was a team of one.
By working together, we can all have lots of fun."

The kids combined their bags, and then they checked to see
What they still needed to bring back to Charity.

Each of them had found many items on the list,
But Flynn was the one who noticed what they had missed.

"The rainbow pinecone," said Flynn, pointing to the sky.
"On Knotty Pine Tree?" said Will. "That is way too high."

"Oh, noodles," said Bunny, "we'll never get it down!"
Sophie shook her head, and her sad face wore a frown.

A bright idea sparked in Bandit's quick-thinking mind.
"I know what to do," he said. "We aren't in a bind.

We've come too far together to give up and stop.
The way to bring it down is by reaching the top."

Working as a team, the kids launched
Bandit in the air.

His hands grabbed the pinecone as
he floated up there.

"We did it!" the kids cheered.
"Working together is fun."

Bandit said to his friends,
"Hey, we got the list all done!"

26

Back at Mystic Lake, Charity raised her voice loud. "Thanks to all my friends," she said. "You all made me so proud.

You worked together as a team, to share and to play, And because you did so, we celebrate this day."

28

The kids made special music with the things they had found.
Bandit was the leader as they marched and danced around.

"The concert is a success," said Bandit happily.
Beautiful music filled the air throughout Willowbe.

29

And that's how Bandit came to finally understand
How teamwork and friendship really do go hand in hand."
Papa Rango gently closes his book for the night,
His smiling face glowing in the warm campfire light.
A pinecone takes shape on Bent Willow Tree,
Remembering a story full of glee.

Laughter and warmth
Surround the campfire

In Willowbe Woods,
Where stories inspire.

The End

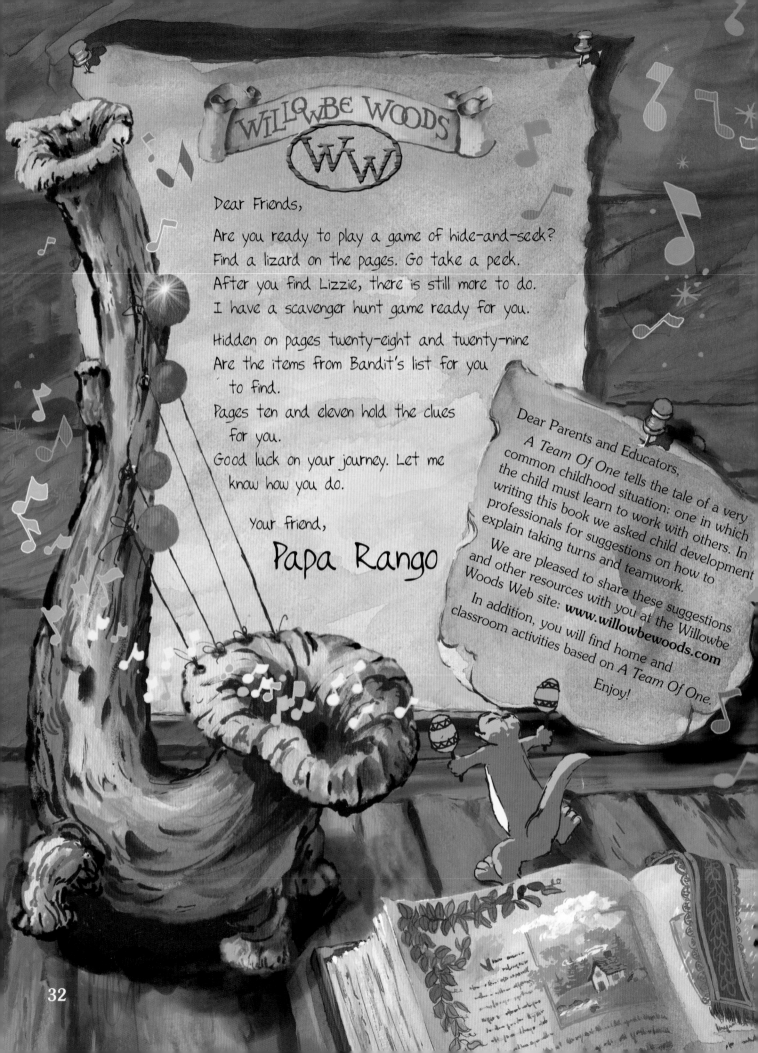

# WILLOWBE WOODS
## WW

Dear Friends,

Are you ready to play a game of hide-and-seek?
Find a lizard on the pages. Go take a peek.
After you find Lizzie, there is still more to do.
I have a scavenger hunt game ready for you.

Hidden on pages twenty-eight and twenty-nine
Are the items from Bandit's list for you
   to find.
Pages ten and eleven hold the clues
   for you.
Good luck on your journey. Let me
   know how you do.

Your friend,

Papa Rango

Dear Parents and Educators,

A Team Of One tells the tale of a very common childhood situation: one in which the child must learn to work with others. In writing this book we asked child development professionals for suggestions on how to explain taking turns and teamwork.

We are pleased to share these suggestions and other resources with you at the Willowbe Woods Web site: **www.willowbewoods.com**

In addition, you will find home and classroom activities based on A Team Of One.

Enjoy!